Benny Bakes a Cake

STORY AND PICTURES BY EVE RICE

GREENWILLOW BOOKS • NEW YORK

For Julie and the mud pie counter

Library of Congress
Cataloging in Publication Data
Rice, Eve.
Benny bakes a cake.
Summary: When the dog eats
Benny's birthday cake,
Daddy comes to the rescue.
[1. Birthdays–Fiction.
2. Cake–Fiction]
I. Title.
PZ7.R3622Be [E] 80-17313
ISBN 0-688-80312-1
ISBN 0-688-84312-3 (lib. bdg.)

For Benny's birthday,
Ralph gives Benny a big wet kiss.

Papa says, "Good morning, Benny.
Happy birthday!"
and goes to town with JoJo.

Mama gives him a hug.
"Happy birthday, birthday boy!
I am going to make your cake.
Will you help me bake it?"

So Benny helps to bake the cake.
Benny sifts

and Benny stirs

and Benny makes sure Ralph is good.

Then the cake goes in the oven,

till finally, it's done.

Mama sets it out to cool.
"Now we have to ice the cake."

So Benny helps to make the icing.
Benny pours

and Benny scrapes.

And Benny watches Ralph
while Mama spreads the icing

on the cake and writes,
"Happy Birthday Benny" very big.

"There! All finished." Mama smiles.
And Benny smiles.
Ralph licks his lips.

Then Mama says,
"We still have time to take a walk."

So Mama slips her apron off.
And Benny gets out his shoes.

But where is Ralph?

There is Ralph!
And <u>there</u> is Benny's cake!

"Bad Ralph, bad dog!" Mama scolds.

But Benny doesn't say a thing—
he just cries.

The telephone goes, "Rrrinnggg. Rrrinnggg!"
"Hello, Papa," Mama says.

"An awful thing
has happened.
Ralph has eaten
Benny's cake...
Why, yes!
Of course!"
And then she says,
"Good-bye."

"Don't cry. It will be all right—you'll see."
Mama hugs Benny tight.
And Ralph is very sorry too.
But Benny cries and will not stop.

Then suddenly, at the door,
"Knock, knock!"
And Papa calls,
"We're here! We're here!
Someone open up!"

Benny stops, wipes his eyes,
and opens up the door...

"Surprise!"

And then, for Benny's birthday,
everybody sings:

"Happy birthday, dear Benny,
Happy birthday to you!"

And it <u>is</u> a happy birthday too.